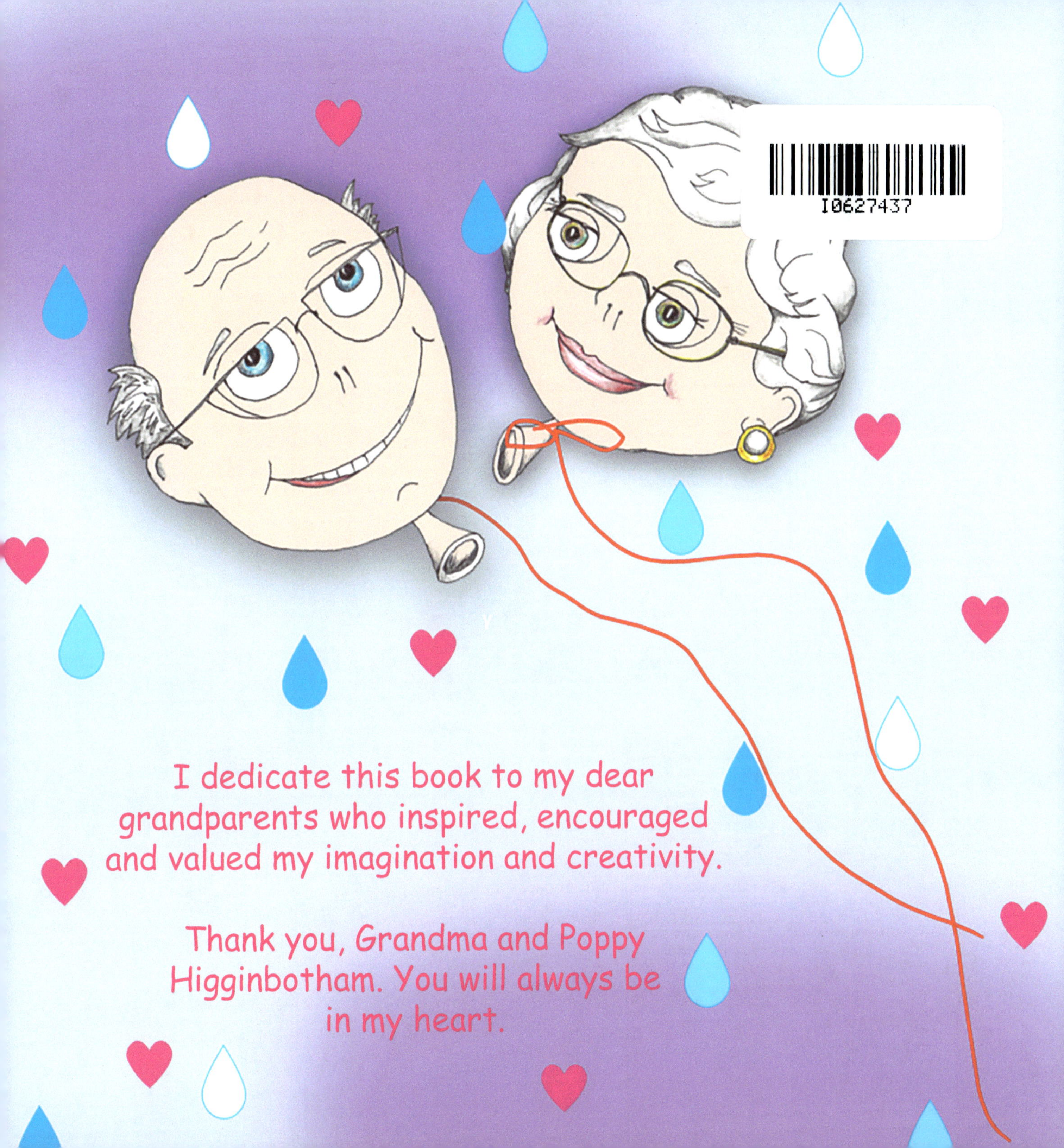


I dedicate this book to my dear
grandparents who inspired, encouraged
and valued my imagination and creativity.

Thank you, Grandma and Poppy
Higginbotham. You will always be
in my heart.

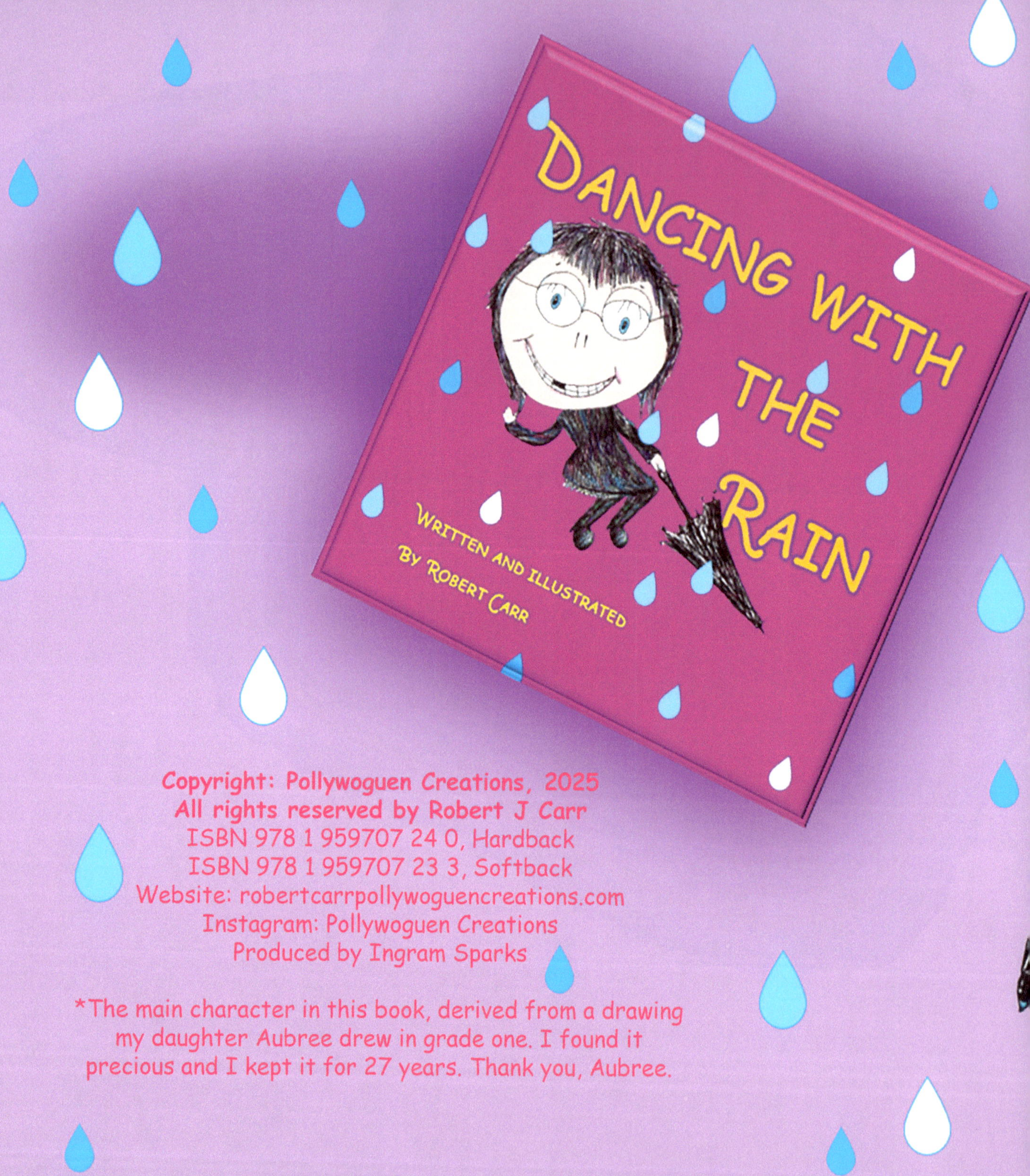

DANCING WITH THE RAIN
WRITTEN AND ILLUSTRATED BY ROBERT CARR

My name is Aubree. I use to dance in the rain until...

One day, Poppy said, "It's raining cats and dogs!"

Grandma said, "One day in your life, it will surely rain frogs!"

At that very moment,
my imagination began
to rain under my hair
and inside my brain.
Now, I dance with
the rain!

# Now, I let it rain dragons and ponies

and wagons and macaronis.

I let it rain bats and French fries

and hats and butterflies.

I let it rain pillows and snails

and armadillos in pails.

I let it rain racoons in clams

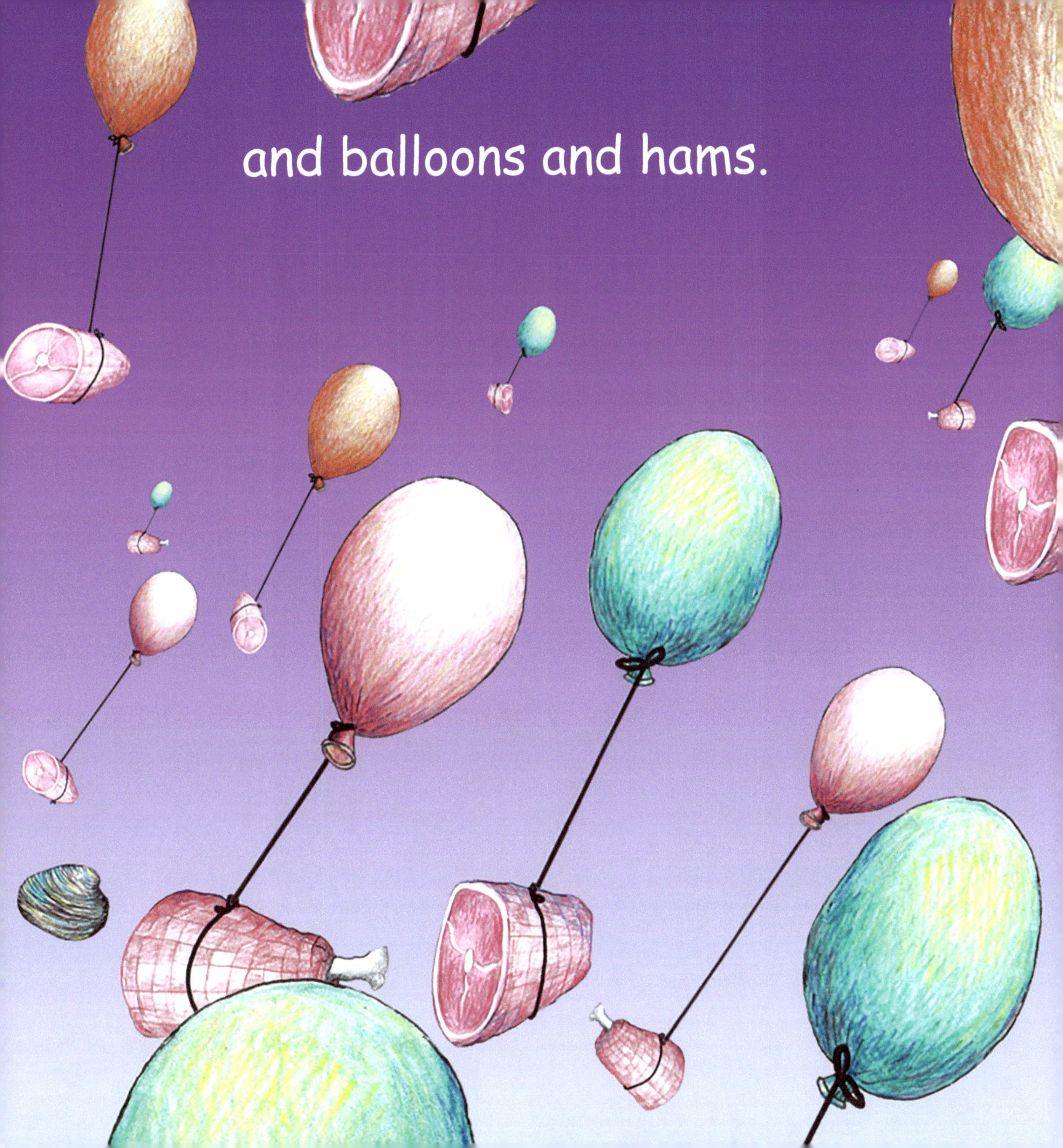
and balloons and hams.

I let it rain sports cars and loons

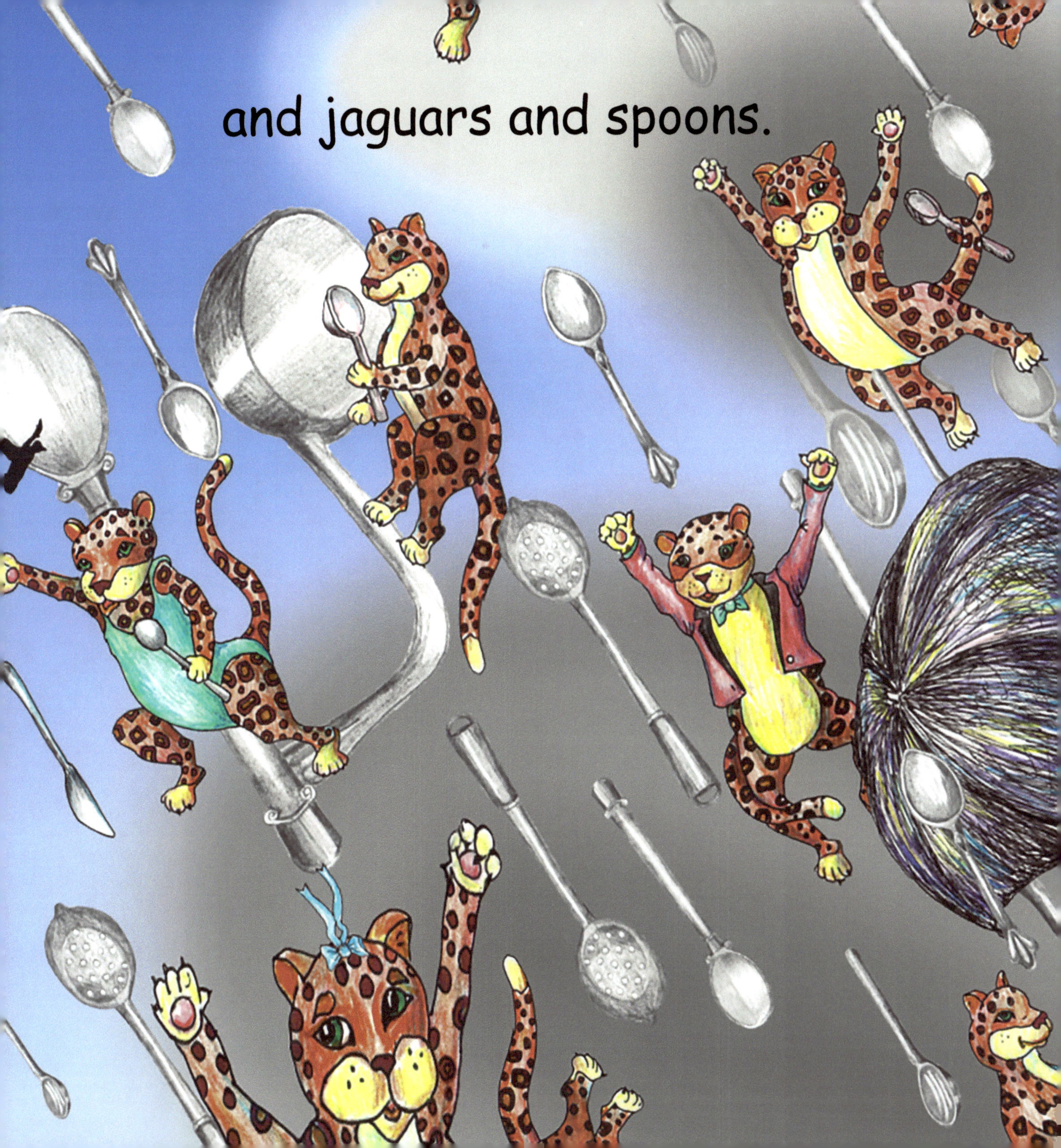
and jaguars and spoons.

I let it rain roots and dogs

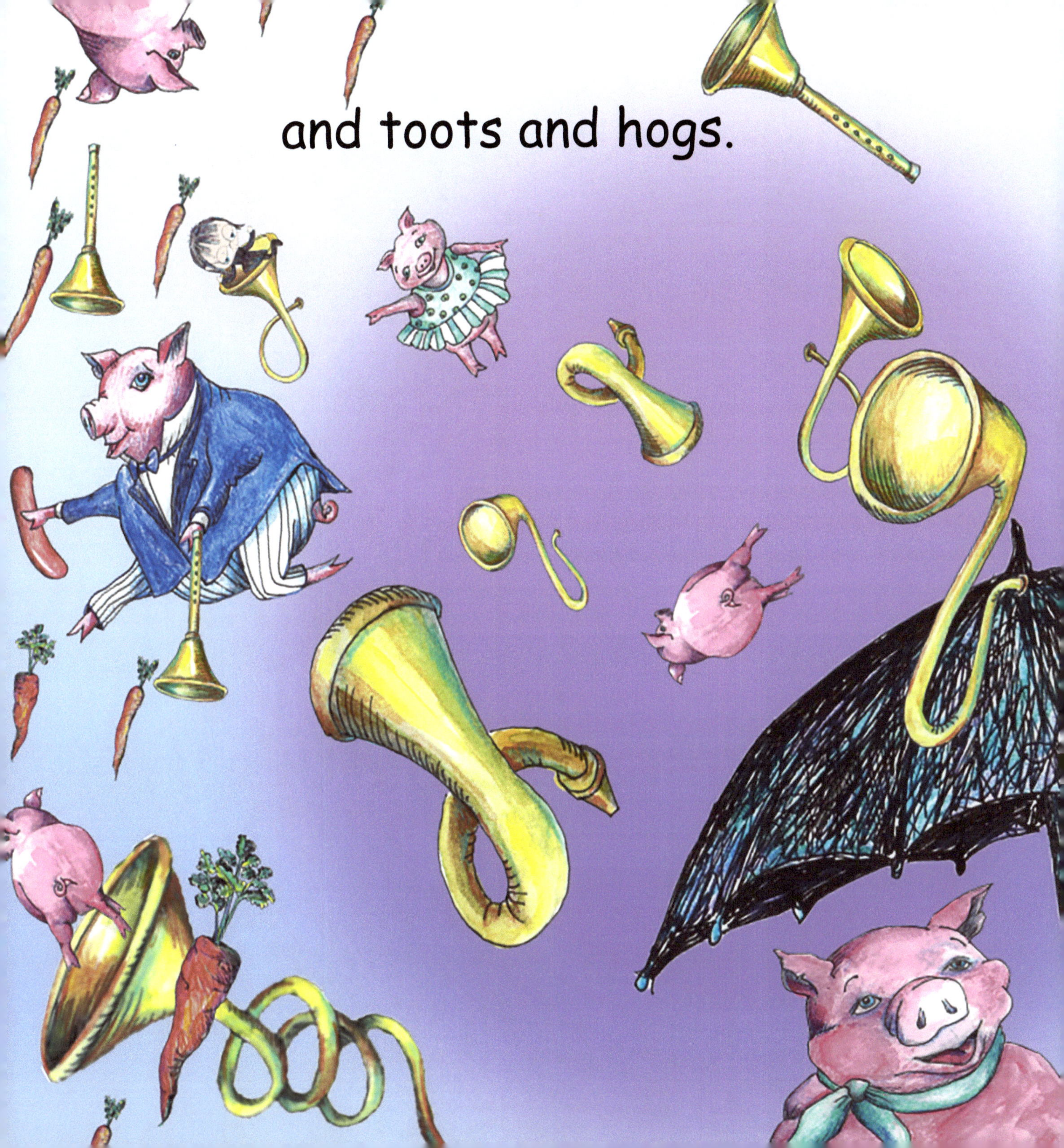
and toots and hogs.

I let it rain lizards and nectarines

and wizards and sardines.

I let it rain cookie jars
COOKIES
COO

and bubblegum stars.

I let it rain snakes and trunks

and cakes and skunks.

I let it rain cats in sandals

and rats and candles.

I just love dancing with my imagination in the rain and in my brain. Many thanks to my Grandma and Poppy. Might you give it a try?

"One day in your life it
will surely rain frogs."

"Night - night."

Other Picture Books by Robert Carr
I Lost My Tooth
Written and Illustrated by Robert Carr

All About Rainbows
Written and Illustrated by Robert Carr


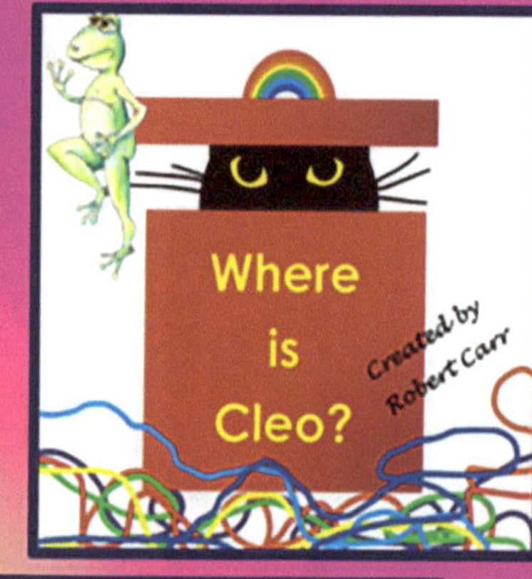

Where is Cleo?
Created by Robert Carr


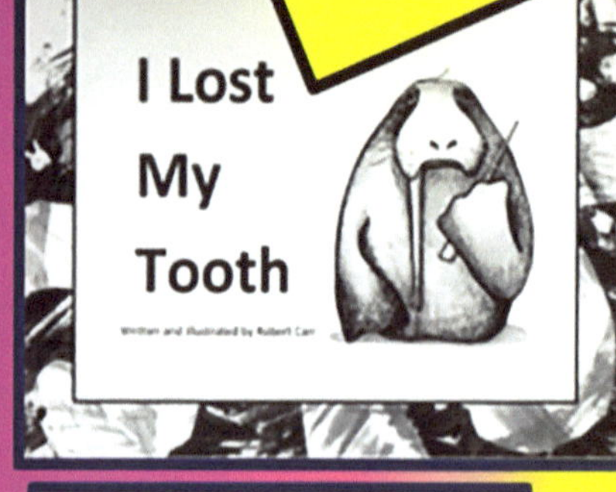

Walrus, Will You Hang With Me?
Written and Illustrated by Robert Carr


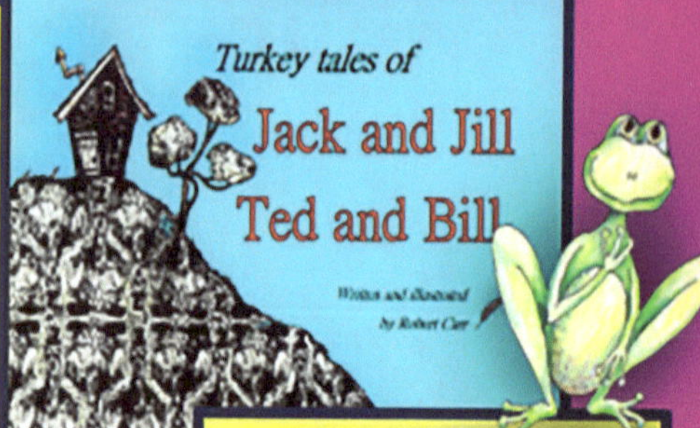

Turkey tales of
Jack and Jill
Ted and Bill
Written and Illustrated
by Robert Carr


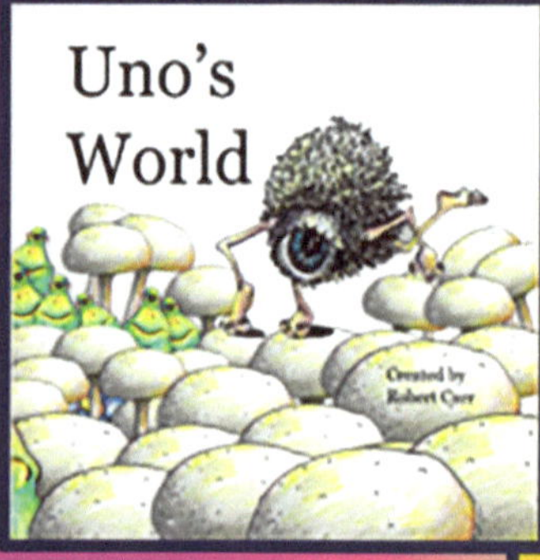

Uno's World
Created by Robert Carr


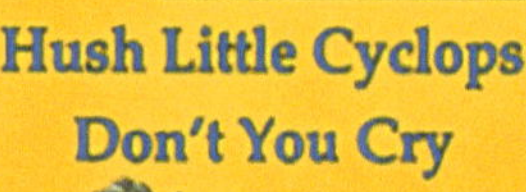

Hush Little Cyclops
Don't You Cry
Written and illustrated by Robert Carr

I am.
Created by Robert Carr

PENCILS COUNT
Created by Robert Carr

Who on Earth am I?
Created by Robert Carr

Pencil Talk
Created by Robert Carr

KELLOGG'S CALENDAR


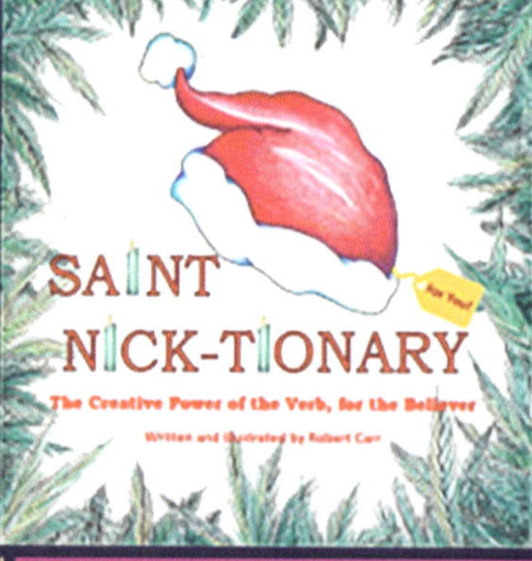

SAINT NICK-TIONARY
The Creative Power of the Verb, for the Believer
Written and Illustrated by Robert Carr